THE LITTLE MERMAID

Adapted by Barbara Bazaldua

Illustrated by the Disney Storybook Art Team

Random House 🏠 New York

rhcbooks.com

ISBN 978-0-7364-3896-4

MANUFACTURED IN CHINA

10 9 8 7 6 5 4 3

Deep under the sea, the merfolk and sea creatures hurried to King Triton's glittering palace. Ariel, the king's youngest daughter, was going to sing in her first concert, and no one wanted to miss it.

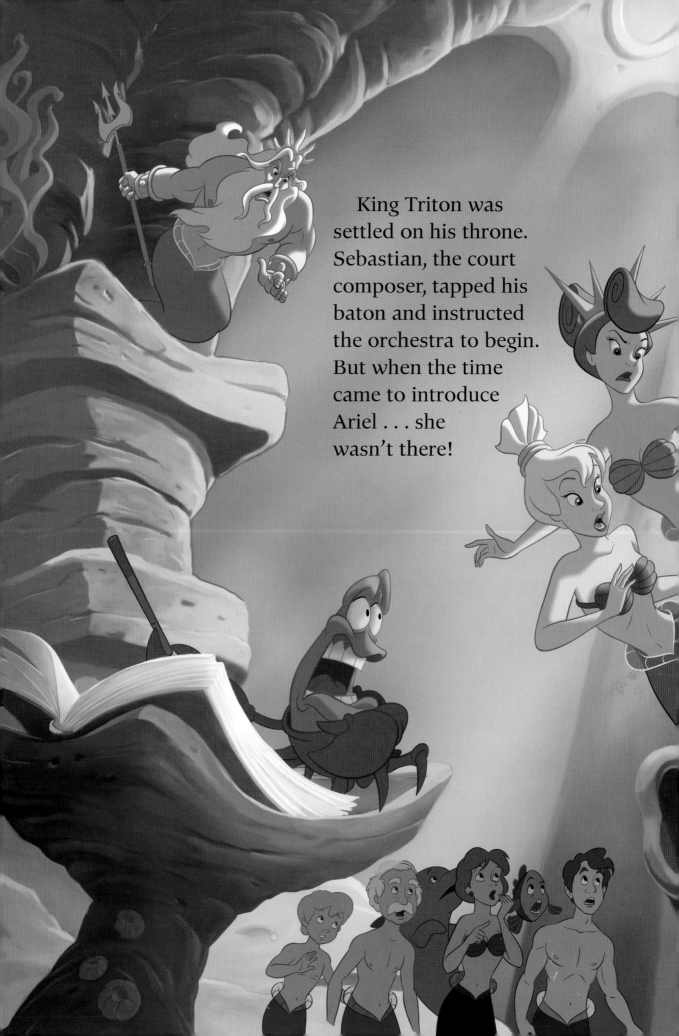

King Triton was
settled on his throne.
Sebastian, the court
composer, tapped his
baton and instructed
the orchestra to begin.
But when the time
came to introduce
Ariel . . . she
wasn't there!

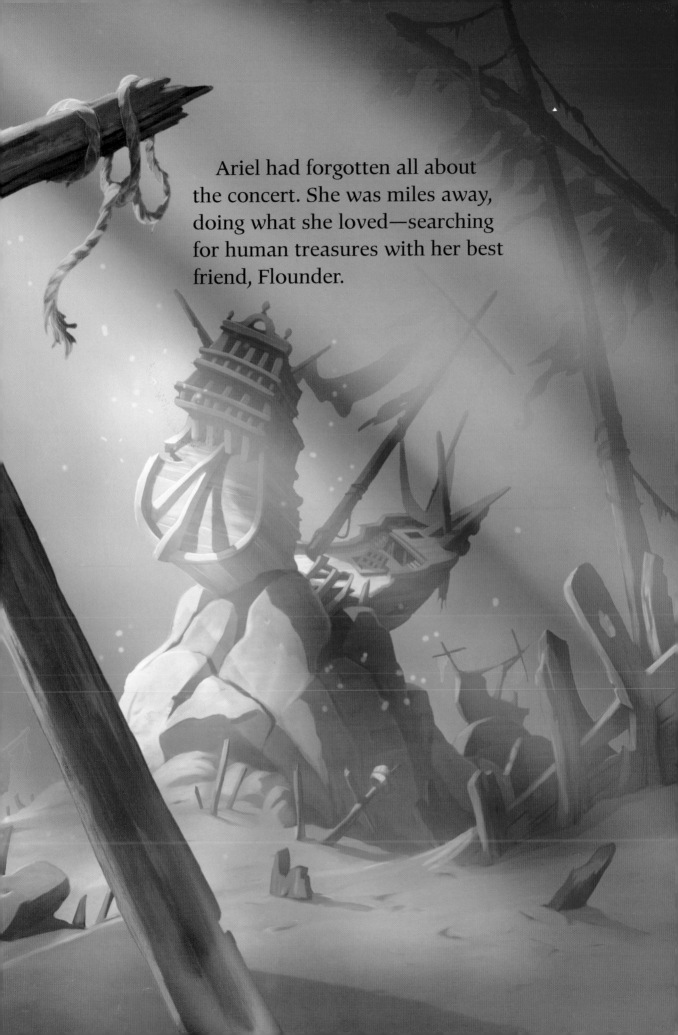

Ariel had forgotten all about
the concert. She was miles away,
doing what she loved—searching
for human treasures with her best
friend, Flounder.

Ariel and Flounder explored a sunken ship.

"Have you ever seen anything so wonderful in your entire life?" Ariel asked with a gasp as she held up a silver fork.

"Yeah, it's great," Flounder muttered. "Now let's get out of here." Flounder was always a bit nervous about being far from home.

Ariel and Flounder swam to the surface to find Scuttle, a silly seagull who claimed to know all about the human world.

"This is a dinglehopper," Scuttle said as he examined the fork. "Humans use these to straighten their hair."

Just then, Ariel remembered the concert. "My father's gonna kill me!" she cried, and she quickly swam home.

When King Triton learned that Ariel had missed the concert because she had gone to the surface, he was furious! He believed humans were dangerous.

"You are never to go to the surface again!" he commanded.

As Ariel sulked and swam away, the king asked Sebastian to keep an eye on his daughter.

Sebastian followed Ariel and Flounder to a secret grotto filled with human treasures.

"I don't see how a world that makes such wonderful things could be bad," Ariel said to Flounder.

Then the little crab overheard Ariel say how much she wanted to be part of the human world. Sebastian was horrified. He tried to talk some sense into Ariel, but it was no use.

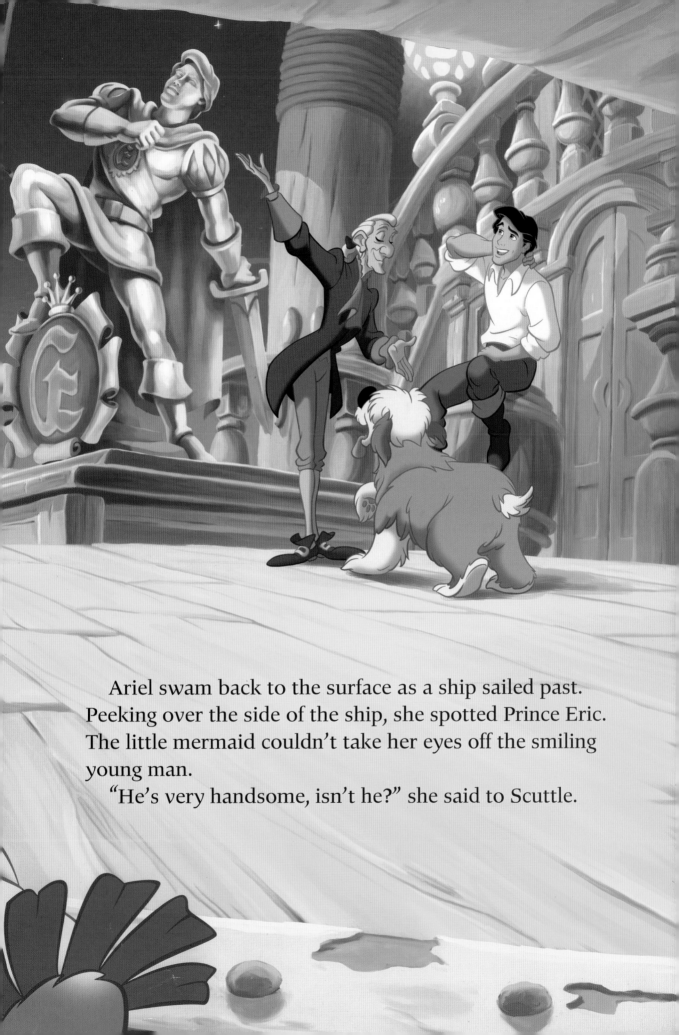

Ariel swam back to the surface as a ship sailed past. Peeking over the side of the ship, she spotted Prince Eric. The little mermaid couldn't take her eyes off the smiling young man.

"He's very handsome, isn't he?" she said to Scuttle.

Suddenly, a fierce storm struck. A lightning bolt set the ship on fire—and a huge wave swept Eric into the sea!

Ariel managed to pull the unconscious prince to shore. She sang to comfort him until the sounds of approaching humans made her dive back under the water.

Eric only caught a glimpse of Ariel's face, but he knew he would remember her beautiful voice forever.

The next day, Ariel swam around in a daze. She was in love! King Triton followed Sebastian to his daughter's grotto. He watched in a rage as Ariel sang to the statue of Eric that had fallen from the ship. "Contact between the human world and the merworld is strictly forbidden!" he thundered.

When Ariel confessed her love for Eric, Triton used his trident to destroy all her treasures.

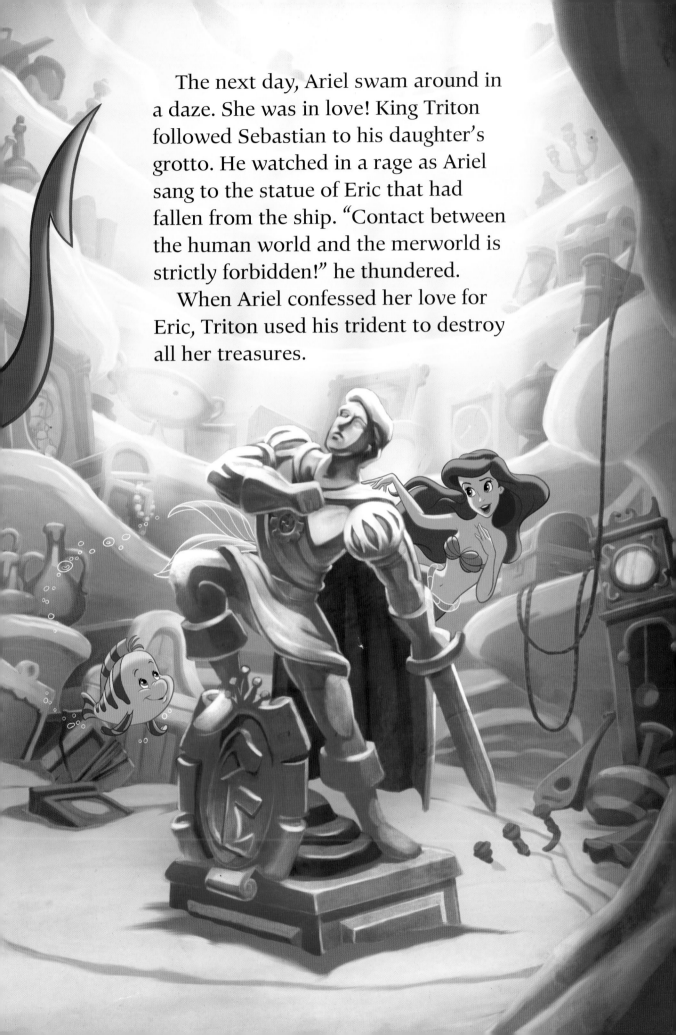

Heartbroken, Ariel went to see Ursula the sea witch. Ursula promised to make the little mermaid human in exchange for her voice. But there was a catch: Eric had to kiss Ariel before sunset on the third day.

"If not, you'll turn back into a mermaid and belong to me!" Ursula cackled.

Ariel was frightened but determined. She agreed to sign Ursula's contract.

Ursula ordered Ariel to sing. The little mermaid's
beautiful voice was captured in a seashell. Then her tail
disappeared. In its place, she had legs!

Quickly, Flounder and Sebastian rushed her to the
surface and helped her to shore.

Ariel was delighted with her new legs, but Sebastian was worried—should he tell King Triton? The softhearted crab knew Ariel would be miserable without Eric, so he promised to help her win the prince's heart. Flounder and Scuttle said they would help, too.

"If you want to be human, you have to dress like one," Scuttle explained. He and Sebastian wrapped Ariel in a ragged old sail.

Just then, Eric's dog, Max, bounded across the beach. The prince followed close behind.

"You look familiar," Eric told Ariel. But when he realized she couldn't speak, he knew that she wasn't the girl with the beautiful voice who had rescued him and sung to him.

Eric took Ariel to his palace, where his friendly servants cared for her. They cleaned her up and gave her a lovely gown to wear. Ariel looked beautiful when she entered the great hall to join Eric and Sir Grimsby for dinner. The prince was speechless!

During dinner, Eric and Grimsby were amazed to see
Ariel comb her hair with a fork. They didn't even notice
Sebastian peeking out from her platter. Eric thought
Ariel was charming and invited her to spend the next
day with him.

The following day, Ariel had a wonderful time exploring Eric's kingdom—but there was no kiss!

As day turned to night, Eric took Ariel rowing in a lagoon. While they floated, Sebastian—with the help of other animal friends—orchestrated a love song.

Prince Eric gazed at Ariel. He leaned closer . . . closer . . . his lips almost touching hers, and . . .

SPLASH! Ursula's nasty eels, Flotsam and Jetsam, tipped the boat over. Eric and Ariel fell into the water before they could kiss. And there was only one day left!

Down in her cavern, Ursula was watching everything in her magic bubble. "That was too close," she said. "It's time I took matters into my own hands."

With a nasty laugh, the sea witch transformed herself into a beautiful young woman named Vanessa. Around her neck she wore the seashell that held Ariel's voice.

"Triton's daughter will be mine!" she shrieked.

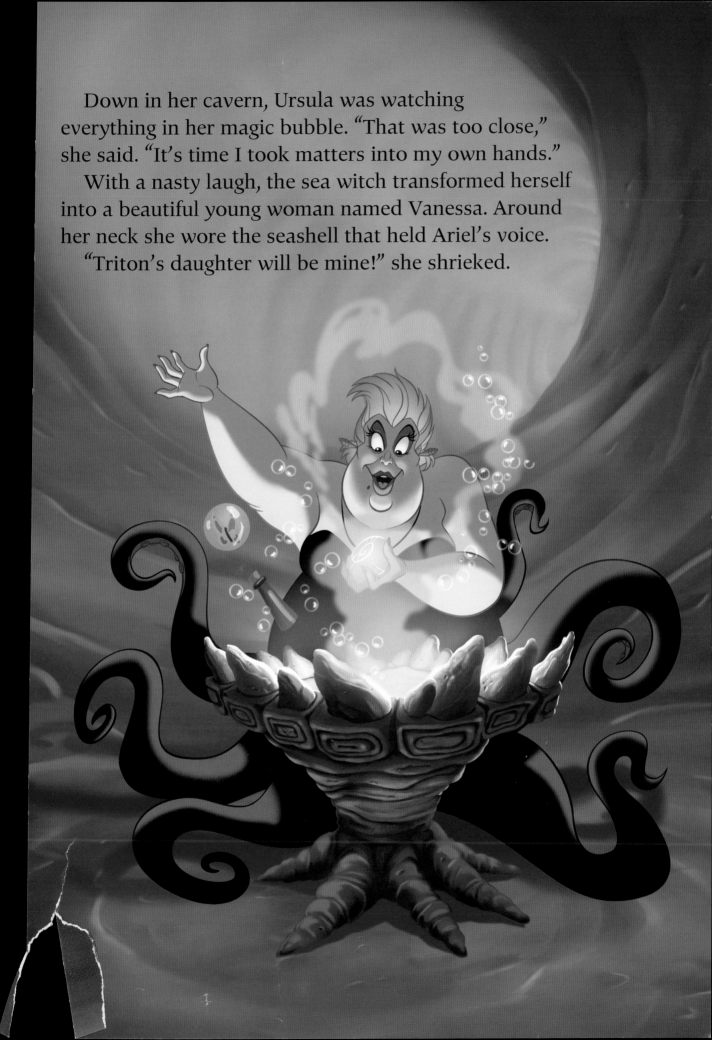

Meanwhile, Eric was on the palace balcony, wondering if he would ever find the mysterious girl with the beautiful voice. Suddenly, he saw Vanessa and heard her sing with Ariel's voice. The prince instantly fell under her spell.

The next morning, Scuttle woke Ariel and congratulated her. He had overheard that Eric was getting married that very day. Ariel was ecstatic until she learned the truth: Eric was marrying Vanessa!

"The wedding ship departs at sunset," Eric told Grimsby in a dull, lifeless voice.

Ariel cried. Not only had she lost her true love, she would become Ursula's slave!

Once aboard the wedding ship, Ursula laughed wickedly. She thought her plan was working perfectly.

She didn't notice Scuttle peeking through the porthole. He saw her true reflection in the mirror and rushed to tell Ariel. "The prince is marrying the sea witch in disguise!" he cried.

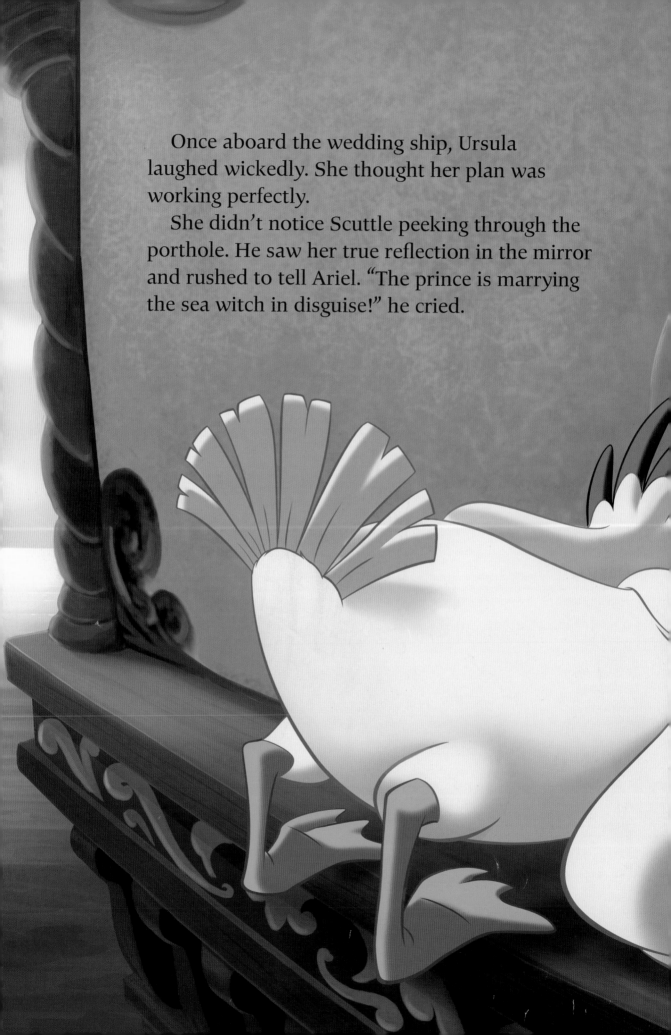

They had to stop the wedding! Ariel clung to a barrel, and Flounder towed her toward the ship. Sebastian raced to find King Triton. Scuttle asked for help from as many friends as he could find.

The sun was going down on the third day. They had to move fast!

The wedding had already begun. But before Vanessa could say her vows, Scuttle and his friends came to the rescue. Birds yanked Vanessa's hair. Dolphins sprayed her with water. Scuttle pulled the shell necklace from her neck. As the seashell shattered, Ariel's voice flowed back to her. The little mermaid could speak!

"Eric?" she said at last.

Finally, Eric was released from the spell. "You're the one!"
he exclaimed to Ariel. But it was too late. The sun sank beneath
the horizon before they could kiss.

Ariel turned back into a mermaid. With a flash of lightning,
Vanessa transformed into Ursula and pulled Ariel into the sea.

King Triton appeared and ordered Ursula to release his daughter.

"She's mine now," Ursula said, showing him the signed contract. "Of course, I might be willing to make an exchange."

To save his daughter, Triton agreed to take Ariel's place as Ursula's servant—which was exactly what the sea witch had wanted all along. Ariel watched in horror as her father shriveled away.

Ursula grew larger and larger. She used the king's trident to stir the waves into violent whirlpools. "Now I am ruler of all the ocean!" she declared.

Luckily, Eric had a plan. He climbed aboard a sunken ship that was rising in the waters and steered its jagged bow through the sea witch's heart. With a howl, Ursula disappeared—and her spell was broken. King Triton and all the others she had tricked were free at last.

But Ariel was a mermaid and could never live on land with Eric. King Triton watched his daughter gaze longingly toward the shore and her true love. With a sigh, he touched his trident to the water, and Ariel became human once again.

King Triton smiled tenderly as he watched Ariel reunite with Prince Eric. And not long afterward, Ariel's friends and family cheered at her wedding. At last, she was part of the human world she loved. And she would live there happily ever after.